Incognito Mosquito Flies Again!

"High-flying pun!" —*Ladies' Hum Journal*

"He'll boll you over—we're gnat kidding."
                    —*The Saturday Evening Pest*

"Bee-utiful. Just bee-utiful!"
                    —*Better Hives and Gardens*

Incognito Mosquito Flies Again!

by E. A. Hass
illustrated by Don Madden

RANDOM HOUSE 🏠 NEW YORK

Library of Congress Cataloging in Publication Data:
Hass, E. A.
  Incognito Mosquito flies again!
  SUMMARY: The mosquito detective tells a class of FBI agents of his
exploits and encounters with such insect offenders and notables as
Russian Cagey Bees, Goldfungus, Mikhail Baryshnimoth, and Gnat
King Cole. Sequel to "Incognito Mosquito, Private Insective."
  1. Children's stories, American. [1. Mosquitoes—Fiction.
2. Insects—Fiction.   3. Mystery and detective stories]   I. Madden,
Don, ill.   II. Title.
PZ7.H2768Im   1985   [Fic]   84-15889
ISBN: 0-394-86728-9 (pbk.); 0-394-96728-3 (lib. bdg.)

Manufactured in the United States of America
1 2 3 4 5 6 7 8 9 0

To Peter Farserotu

They don't come any better

CONFIDENTIAL

The following information can be released only to individuals with the highest security clearance. But, as long as you've gotten this far . . .

The cases you are about to read come from the files of one Incognito Mosquito, Private Insective. You will learn of bugs so mean that they think the evil Mr. Hive is Dr. Jekyll's better half. You will find thugs so greedy that the only thing they'd share with you is a communicable disease. You will hear of insect fiends so cruel that they make their prisoners eat spaghetti—through a straw.

Only in the files of Incognito Mosquito will you find such tales. Fortunately. Now it's all up to you. So give it a buzz—before you bug out!

The course was listed in the FBI refresher catalog as:

SLIME AND PUN-ISHMENT 3A
A one-day intensive seminar on nipping insect no-goodskies in the bug, presented by one of the nation's foremost slime fighters.

My boss, editor of a famous underground newspaper, thought it would be a good idea for someone to attend the course. As she put it, "When the Federal Bureau of Insectigation squalks, bugs listen." As for why she chose me? We all drew straws to see who would get this assignment, and I guess you could say I drew the short end of it.

Actually, I figured the course might even be interesting. That is, until I opened the classroom door. When I saw who was teaching, it was all I could do to keep my-

self from making a beeline for the exit. The pesty Incognito Mosquito, Private Insective, stood before me big as life.

Unfortunately the drone had already begun. Rather than risking a scene, I took a seat in the back and made myself as comfortable as possible. Closing my eyes, I tried to imagine myself in more pleasant surroundings—say, the dentist's office.

Then I watched with amazement as all of the students craned forward to catch every word rolling off Incognito Mosquito's golden forked tongue. It's true, the Mosquito was well-known as a world-renowned insective able to solve cases considered unsolvable by others. And it's also true, the bug had duped me in my last book, *Incognito Mosquito, Private Insective*. But it wouldn't happen again. Now I was un-dupable. I was determined to get my story this time.

So I sat in a classroom full of students dying to catch everything I.M. said. Never have so many gotten so little from so little! Still, I had to admire the Insective. This Mosquito was hot stuff. Sometimes even too hot to handle. With all of his painfully obvious disabilities, he still managed to solve his cases. Sometimes he actually tripped over them.

I saw that I was right again. In fact, I watched the Mosquito stumble over his own attaché case. Then he made a heroic effort to start a serious lecture while untangling himself from the coil of projector cord he had unwittingly stepped into. "Unwittingly," I laughed to myself. What an appropriate way to describe the Mosquito.

"I want you . . . ugh . . . all to . . . eeh . . . understand that slime fighting is . . . mmh . . . a very serious business," began the Mosquito as he tried to pull his foot

6

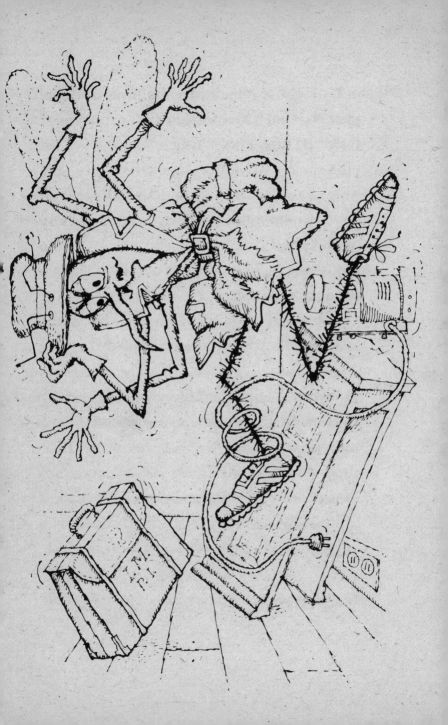

out of the ever tightening noose. "The professional insective must be prepared for everyone, everything, everywhere. My motto is, 'Anyslime, anytime.' By the time . . . ooh, ah . . . you leave this class, you'll understand . . . eeh . . . what it's like to be called by clients at any hour of the day or night. The only private life you have is your private insective life. The only time you can call your own is the same . . . oomph . . . time that they call theirs.

"And this . . . urumph . . . is not going to be an . . . uph . . . fly-by-night course." He huffed and puffed as the tangled cord pulled him to the floor. "However, there was one instance when I, Incognito Mosquito, Private Insective, was called upon to fly by night. And that would be a very good place to start. . . ."

1
The Case of the Foiled Flyjackers

Ah! This is the life, I thought to myself as I sprawled luxuriously in my seat. Here I was, aboard Pun American Airlines on my way to the exotic Orient. I'd chosen the less crowded local route after finding out it's murder to get on the Orient Express and had actually found the trip quite relaxing. I don't know why I'd been putting it off, except that I knew when I left that I would leave a gaping hole. I guess I was afraid someone would just plaster it up and that would be that.

While many of my closest friends had been begging me to go away—far away— for years, it was the Chief, Inspector Insector, who finally convinced me. He got on his hands and knees and begged me to leave. Actually, he suggested that I take a hike.

So anyway, there I was, leafing through the latest *Harper's Buzaar,* listening to the gentle strains of Johann Sebastian Bugg through the headphones, and nibbling on some cheese and crackers. I had just or- dered my usual—a water on the rocks with a Shirley Temple chaser—when suddenly

I heard a loud click. The music snapped off, and a voice came over the headphones.

"Good evening, Mr. Mosquito. This is the captain speaking. Two members of the notorious Russian Cagey Bee, disguised as mild-mannered Chinese business bugs, are on this plane. They were going to flyjack us to their homeland by threatening to blow the plane up. Fortunately we were able to nip their plan in the bug, so to speak. We were tipped off about the bomb hidden in the luggage compartment and removed it. Unfortunately the identities of the two KGB members remain a mystery. Your mission, should you decide to accept it—and you don't have much of a choice—is to accompany this plane on an emergency landing

in Stingapore. Once there, you will attempt to reveal the identities of the two KGB members. This tape will self-destruct in five seconds."

Almost immediately, smoke began to pour out of my ears. "Oh, good!" I thought. "The ole brain is working already." Not until later did I realize the smoke was from the tape self-destructing in my headphones.

I arrived at Stingapore International Airport without further incident. Realizing that it was of utmost importance not to arouse the flyjackers' suspicion, I decided to wear one of my many famous costumes. You know, it's hard to be incognito when you're famous. But that's another story. I selected number 147LSB—my Little Spoiled Brat outfit. It comes complete with hot dog registered at the American Kennel Club. The airport security guards just stood by, waiting for me to make my move.

The airport waiting room was filled with uptight Oriental business bugs of every size, shape, and color, all eager to be released and go about their daily buziness. Most looked nervous enough to lick the beaters with the mixer still running. Little did they know that my photographic mind was snapping candid shots of all of them. I would have been willing to sell them prints at a very reasonable price, but of course I couldn't tell them that. So I kept my mouth shut and my shutter open.

14

You'd be amazed at how much you can learn just by watching. My goal in life is to learn more and more about less and less until one day I'll know everything about nothing. With this in mind, I looked over the passengers. My keen insective eyes searched each one, looking for something suspicious that would give the sly flyjackers away. I watched for the most subtle of gestures, the smallest slip, the tiniest thing amiss—or a mister, for that matter.

I knew that dressed as a kid I could poke around and ask some really outrageous questions that would have rated a punch in the nose or a slap in the face coming from an adult. Like, just for fun, I walked up to this really skinny bug and asked, "Walked through any harps lately?" Then I went up to one of those types whose nose is glued to a mirror and whose hand is glued to a comb and said, "Gee, you have a striking face. Have you been struck often? Run into any good busses lately?"

But enough fun. Getting back to work, I carefully watched every passenger. I knew that somewhere, someway, somehow the KGB flyjackers would give themselves away by standing out in the crowd of Chinese business bugs. Every time I was sure that a passenger was okay, I licked my lollipop. That was my secret sign to airport security that they could release the passenger.

16

Finally there were only a couple of business bugs left. They wore identical dark pinstriped suits and sat quietly reading their Chinese newspapers. In fact, they were so absorbed that they didn't even notice me buzzing around. Their eyes positively raced across the pages. Back and forth. Back and forth. Their baggage tags identified the two bugs as Ho Chi Flea and Mao Tsetse Fly. I tried to get their attention for a few questions, but they didn't even look up. They just brushed me away, muttering something that sounded suspiciously like the Chinese version of "Buzz off, kid. You bother me." Of course, I wouldn't know, since I don't speak Chinese.

I smiled sweetly. The lollipop saw to that. Or could it have been the sweet smell of success? For at that very moment I realized that my photographic mind was about to pay off. Not only was something developing, but I was going to get a full set of prints out of it. Fingerprints, that is! Because I knew that Ho Chi Flea and Mao Tsetse Fly were the culprits.

The notorious KGB members didn't even look up as the airport security guards snapped the half a dozen sets of handcuffs closed. I knew my work in the Orient was done. Another wonton criminal had bitten the dust.

HOW DID INCOGNITO MOSQUITO KNOW WHO THE FLYJACKERS WERE?

In Incognito's own words, "Chinese is all Greek to me." However, even our Insective knew that Chinese is read in a column from the top to the bottom of the page. The two disguised business bugs from Russia were so busy pretending to read their newspapers that they forgot one important item: They were reading Chinese newspapers.

By reading across the page instead of up and down, Mao Tsetse Fly and Ho Chi Flea earned themselves a trip across the ocean and up the river. They were each sentenced to fifteen years at hard labor stuffing misfortune cookies.

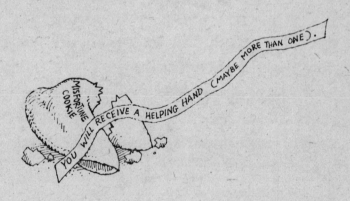

"**S**o you can see, this is one unpredictable business," I.M. said to the class. "You just never know what's waiting for you beyond the next door—" He was interrupted by several knocks. "Or behind the door for that matter." He smiled, casually twisting the doorknob.

But before he could pull open the door, it flew open, pinning the Insective flat against the wall. "Mr. Mosquito, are you here?" asked our visitor.

"In back of the door," the squishee replied flatly. "Ah, it's you, Ladybug," he said, prying himself off the wall. "My loyal

SLIME AND
DUN-ISHMENT
3 A

YOUR
INSTRUCTOR:
INCOGNITO
MOSQUITO, P.I.

secretary," he explained to us. "Come to bring me some top-secret information on a hush-hush rush-rush case, I presume."

"No, actually, you presume wrong on both counts. One: My name is *not*, never has been, never will be, Ladybug. It is, always has been, ever will be, Ms. Womanbug. Two: I came to bring you a summons from the courthouse."

"Oh, nuts!" the Insective exclaimed. "They've finally caught up with that parking ticket, haven't they? It just keeps slipping my mind."

"That and how many other things?" she muttered. "No, no such luck. This summons is from Inspector Insector. He wants you to testify against that fugitive fly you brought in last week. And you know how rough the Inspector can be in court."

"Ah, yes. He gives double cross examinations." The Mosquito nodded. "So once again he wants me as the key witless for the persecution."

"Yes, I suppose you could say that," Ms. Womanbug replied wearily. "You, but only you. And oh yes. The Chief is a little worried. He says you haven't been acting like yourself lately. He's afraid you might start again. Please don't." Ms. Womanbug turned to leave.

"Leaving so soon?" Mosquito asked coyly. "I was hoping you'd help me demonstrate the fine art of self-defense. For example, what would you do if I came at you like this?" asked the Insective, lunging fiercely for Ms. Womanbug's throat.

"I'd do this," she said, calmly tossing Mosquito over her left shoulder.

"A little flip, aren't you?" questioned the tossee.

"It takes pun to know pun," Ms. Womanbug answered smartly. "Ciao."

The dazed Mosquito looked up. "Oh, is it lunchtime already? My, the time does creep up on you, doesn't it? Let's take one more case before we break, shall we? This case will creep up on you too!"

2
The Creeping
Fungus Caper

I was never so surprised as I was the time that infamous insect offender Goldfungus begged for my help. I would lichen the situation to Goliant coming to David. I'm no James Bug, agent 007 you know. And actually, *begged* might not be quite the right word. Terrorized, menaced, threatened with bodily harm is more like it.

It all began like this: I had just thrown my lunch basket into my brand-new Sting-Ray, jumped in myself, and started off for a picnic in the country. I tried to make a right turn, but the car turned left. It took only a second to check. Yes, there was no doubt about it. Right there on my sneaker, it said "left" all right. The car continued to head left, and worse, it speeded up. I was being taken for a ride!

I soon realized that I had absolutely no control over the car. The doors locked, making escape impossible. Someone had obviously tampered with the controls. Fortunately no one had tampered with my hamper. So I decided to just sit back, eat my lunch, and enjoy the ride.

But before I knew it, the picnic was

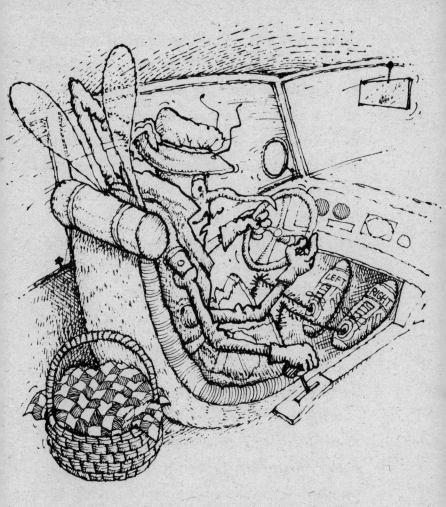

over. The car screeched to a halt. I was
unceremoniously pulled out by a thug and

dumped down a long dark chute. Finally I exited onto a bumpy floor and was greeted by dozens of pairs of solid-gold sneakers, all in a row. What Bugs Bunny would have done for all those carats! My insective mind was off and running. Sneakers? What goes into sneakers? Athlete's feet! P.U.! And what goes into gold sneakers? Gold athlete's feet! Immediately I had my answer. All of those sneakers could belong to none other than my old adversary, Goldfungus. A real stinker! And the sneakiest sneaker of them all!

I looked up and, sure enough, there he was. At first I thought Goldfungus was looking down on me. Then I realized that all of the gold chains around his neck (what neck?) made his head tilt. He seemed all the more crooked to me!

"Sorry for the rough ride. But that's shoe business," Goldfungus said with a sneer.

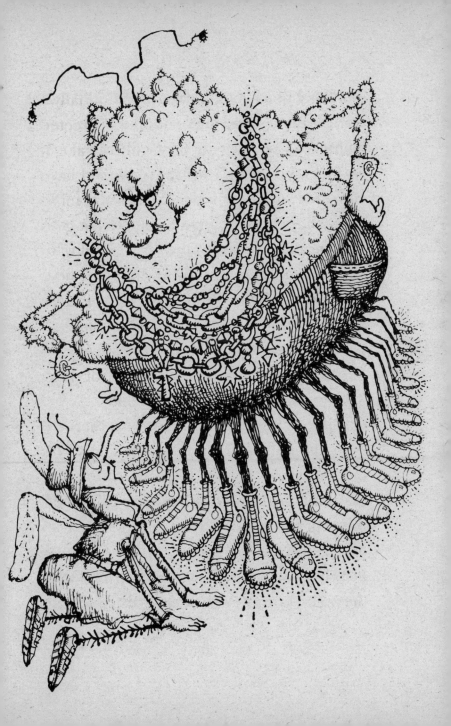

"Talk about your golden moldies! That one creeps up and hits you like a sludge-hammer. Come on now, Goldfungus," I coaxed. "You didn't bring me here to discuss the leather." I waited patently for the other shoe to drop. I hadn't expected to see Goldfungus for a very long time. "I thought you'd been sentenced to two hundred and fifty years or life—whichever came last—for kidnapping, robbery, blackmail, forgery, counterfeiting, auto theft, and jay (k,l,m . . .) walking."

"I got time off for good behavior," he explained. "Listen, Mosquito, we gotta talk. That international fly ring, Interpod, is after me. Its leader, Fidel Cockroach, found out that I double-crossed the gang to get out of prison a few decades early. I'm due to testify against them in a few days. You gotta help me, Mosquito. They're after me. And the police don't believe it. They keep telling me that the bad guys only go after the good guys. Mosquito, if Interpod gets me, the court will be out one star witness, and I'll be out for good!"

"Hold it, hold it," I said calmly. "What makes you so sure it's Interpod that has a contract out on you? You didn't sign anything, did you?"

"No, don't be ridiculous. I have evidence," the big Fung said triumphantly, pulling a slug from his pocket. "Look at this! It's the slug from the bullet they shot at me. See—it's still moving. I dug it out of the wall only a few minutes ago. Like I said, I'm in serious danger here. You've gotta help me!"

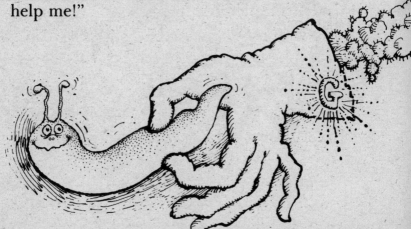

"Okay. Will do, Mildew. But listen. I understand you were in the line of fire. And I'll agree that position is nine tenths of the law. But I still don't understand how Fidel Cockroach and Interpod tie in. Are you sure you're not making a mountain out of an anthill?"

"No, Mosquito, I'm positive about this. I've got definite proof. As you remember, I'm a serious believer in astrology. Well, that's how I knew something was going to happen even before it did," Goldfungus said with a starry look in his eyes. "The whole day started off terribly. First thing, I went to see my medium, Miss Tic. She's not bad, for a medium, and you know, good mediums are rare. Anyway, she read my future in the tea leaves. She told me that someone would attack me, that I was in great danger, and that I might even be killed!"

"That's quite a horrorscope you've got

there." I nodded sympathetically. I had to admit, Goldfungus was beginning to grow on me.

"So anyway," Goldfungus continued, "right to begin with I was on my guard— my right guard that is. My medium turned out to be worth her weight in tarot cards. I'd just turned the corner from Pollywog onto Vine when I heard something I thought was a giggle. Someone was following me! All of a sudden a shot rang out behind me from around the corner. What a dingdong I was, leaving myself exposed like that! Fortunately, though, the bullet just missed me. The slug I dug out of the wall is proof of that. So that's how I know that Fidel Cockroach and Interpod are after me."

"Hold on there, Goldfungus," I said. "You seem to have forgotten one little item. Under the law, a bug is innocent until proved guilty. You may have proof that someone shot at

you, but you don't have proof of *who* shot at you. Tell me, did you actually see who did it?"

"Why, Mosquito, dear friend. I think you doubt my word! It's true that I could only see the tip of the gun, but I assure you that I can positively identify the culprit as Fidel Cockroach. You see, I'd know that laugh anywhere."

"Ah ha!" I said. "Well, you know the old saying: He who laughs last laughs first . . . or is that he who laughs first laughs last, or . . . Well, whoever laughs whenever, Goldfungus, the laugh is on you. You've just let Fidel Cockroach off the hook. Now the shoe's on the other heel!" I knew that no one had shot at Goldfungus. His attempt to sting Fidel Cockroach and Interpod had backfired! I folded my arms across my chest, waiting for a response.

Goldfungus was speechless. So much for

my supposedly honest, straightlaced arch-enemy! Now all I had to do was figure out how to untangle my arms so that I could shake my own hand and pat myself on the back.

HOW DID INCOGNITO MOSQUITO KNOW THAT GOLDFUNGUS WAS OUT TO STING FIDEL COCKROACH AND INTERPOD?

HERE'S HOW:

Unfortunately for Goldfungus, the gun that he described was nowhere near as crooked as he was. Since Goldfungus (the shootee) had just turned the corner, Fidel Cockroach (the supposed shooter) would have had to turn the corner too—and so would have been in full view behind him. Guns can't shoot around the corner. If his story were on the level, Goldfungus would have seen the entire gun as well as Cockroach himself. Yet Goldfungus claimed that he could only see the tip of the gun.

How Goldfungus claimed it happened.

The only way shooting could have happened.

Goldfungus figured he could score some points with the judge if she thought he was risking his life to testify against Interpod. And by trying to frame Fidel Cockroach and the guys, risking his life is just what he did.

While the frame-up that Goldfungus had staged was not grounds to send him back to prison, Incognito knew it was only a matter of slime before he slipped up. And to quote the Mosquito himself, "You know how slime passes when you're having pun."

At that point the class broke for lunch. Naturally we had ordered the Incognito Mosquito Special—half turkey, half ham: on white bread (with the crusts cut off) for the wasps, on hero submarine rolls for those brave bugs in the FBI underwater squad, on open sesame (seed) buns for the rest of us, with extra "mayo" for the medical corps.

As we headed for the cafeteria with Incognito Mosquito in the lead, he continued his talk. "Now, I want you students to understand that this private insective game is no picnic. Oh, sure, we have ants, but doesn't everybody? Yes, we come face-to-face with danger at every turn."

At just that moment we rounded the corner onto a corridor clearly marked FRESHLY WASHED FLOOR. However, I guess clearly is in the eye of the beholder and no matter how hard we tried, we couldn't be holding Incognito Mosquito from losing his footing and sliding down the hall at breakneck speed. Breaking his neck is one of the few things that the Mosquito didn't do.

Finally the Mosquito stepped on the bottom of a soaking wet mop, which flew up and smacked him in the nose. Momentarily stunned, I.M. grabbed the mop to steady himself. He took a few tentative dance steps with it, then came to his senses (such as they are).

"Uhm, ahem, ooohoo! Dow as I was sayig, danger ad ebery durn. See whad I bean?" he said, trying to straighten out the broomhandle-shaped indentation in his dose. I mean nose. "Ooh, my!" continued Mosquito, more dazed than usual. "Ab I seeing stars! Loog at dem dancing above by head. Whig rebinds be of anoder story."

3
The Mis-cast Dancer Mystery

I had just taken my seat at the ballet and was looking forward to a terrific evening. This was the gala premiere of the St. Vitus Dance Troupe's newest production, *The Grasshopper Suite*. My date was the

stunning Lorna Larvae. We were celebrat-
ing her coming out, and she was ripe for
the picking. The orchestra began its over-
ture and I began mine. Proceeding slowly,
I wrapped my arms around the back of
Lorna's seat. These things have to be done
delicately. Extra arms can come in handy,
you know. It was at times like this that I
wished I'd been born a millipede!

Just then, I felt a slap on my shoulder. Rejection already? I glanced over at the seat next to mine. The glorious Miss Larvae had disappeared. This was her coming-out party. Had she gone back in already? I wondered. In her chair was the Chief, Inspector Insector, who practically dragged me out of my seat and into the lobby. Fortunately I was able to quickly untangle my arms from the chair. Otherwise I would have lost a few and my loss would have been the chair's gain. I've heard of armchairs, but that would have been ridiculous.

"I'd really like to make this an open-and-shut case, Mosquito," the Chief said under his breath. "As soon as you open your mouth, I'd like to shut this door in your face. But it seems that the ballet master, one Mr. R. Abesque, thinks you have culture and taste. Little does he know that your taste is all in your mouth."

"Well, actually, Chief, he's not too far off. I have always considered myself a peon of the arts."

The Chief wasted no time, either in listening to me or in explaining what was going on. It seemed that the St. Vitus Dance Troupe wanted to present a very valuable gold medal to the world-famous dancer Mikhail Baryshnimoth at a special ceremony following tonight's performance. Mr. Baryshnimoth had indeed arrived on schedule, but somehow something was wrong.

There was some question as to the iden-

tity of the guest. A telegram had arrived earlier explaining that the dancer had to cancel his appearance due to a terrible accident, and yet here was someone claiming to be the great Baryshnimoth himself. There was no way of telling whether this was the real dancer or not! You see, Mr. B. *had* been in this terrible accident recently, so his face was totally bandaged. Also, his left leg was broken, making any dancing out of the question.

So the troupe was faced with the embarrassing predicament of risking the presentation of the medal to an impostor, or canceling the entire ceremony and possibly offending what could be the real Baryshnimoth. The Chief was faced with an even more embarrassing predicament—calling me.

But as usual, he handled the situation with great tact. That's one thing you have to say for the Inspector. He's very tacky. The Chief explained that in order not to arouse suspicion, I was to be introduced as the ballet critic for that snobbish dance magazine *Too-Too*. Then we went backstage to meet either one of the world's greatest dancers or a very clever impostor.

And clever he was. The supposed Mr. Baryshnimoth was charming but sneaky. The Chief was right. The dancer's face was totally bandaged, and his left leg was in a cast to his hip. He leaned heavily on the crutch under his right wing. Every traditional means of identification was a dead end. We chatted casually about the dance, but this bug pulled off his ballet ruse well. He went through all of the positions, really kept me on my toes.

To be honest, I myself have never really understood the principles of ballet. I've never gotten the "pointe" of it, so to speak.

I mean, if they want bigger ballerinas, why don't they just get girls a foot taller instead of making them walk around on their toes all the time? And if the girls weren't wearing themselves out by walking around on tiptoe, the boys wouldn't always

have to pick them up and carry them all over the place. This would leave a lot more time for dancing, don't you think? When I asked the alleged Baryshnimoth to explain this, for my readers of course, he looked confused.

The Chief didn't look confused. He turned bright red and muttered, "Mosquito, I don't understand why you call yourself a private insective. Public defective is more like it!" It was then that I realized I'd made a pas de faux. Or is that a faux de pas? No matter, it takes deux to tango. Any dancer knows that.

All this time, the ballet had been proceeding on schedule. Dancers whisked by us in tu-tus, three-threes, and four-fours, clad in multicolored tights (and looses), doing arabesques and araworsques, pliés and pliebies. It was growing dangerously close to presentation time, time for the case's finale, and for me to bow out gracefully. There was just one problem—I still had not solved the mystery. Was the bug standing before me an invalid impostor or an innocent invalid? I just wasn't sure. I began to wonder if this was to be my farewell appearance, my swan song, whether I had pirou-ed my last ette.

Then suddenly an idea hit me like a ton of bricks. Or like a sandbag. Actually, it *was* a sandbag. I'd accidentally bumped into the rope that held the bag high above the stage, thereby triggering its (and my) downfall. Excusing myself, I headed dizzily for the little bugs' room and whipped out my Newly Perfected, Highly Effective Insective Detective Kit the moment I was out of sight.

Without wasting a minute (or any more than I'd already wasted), I grabbed the bottle I was looking for and began to rub the

clear liquid on my palms. A special solution of my own invention, this stuff would harden into a gel that would faithfully record the fingerprints of anyone who shook my hand. Then I could instantly match those fingerprints with the fingerprints of the real Baryshnimoth. There was just one bug in the system . . . but I'll get to that later. Now it was time to catch a fly in my ointment. (A moth actually, but I'm not picky.) I ran backstage, prepared to leave my mark on the Baryshnimoth case. Or to have Baryshnimoth leave his mark on me.

The Chief was where I'd left him, making small talk with the dancer. The Inspector is known for his tremendous presence of mind at times like this. He has often also commented on my absence of brain.

"I just wanted to applaud Mr. Baryshnimoth," I explained, while clapping my hands. "And also to shake the wing of a great dancer." At that point I tried to extend my right hand, but that was where the trouble started. I had forgotten the stickiness effect of my potion if not used immediately. In the few minutes since I'd applied it, the stuff had stuck my hands together. The more I pulled, the stickier it got. I tried frantically to wipe the stuff off,

but you know what they say—"If the glue
fits, wear it." In this case I didn't have much
of a choice.

The Chief stepped forward looking ready
to explode. "Mosquito, don't ever let any-

one tell you that you're a stupid, incompetent fool. I want to be the one to tell you!"

Fortunately, at that moment the supposed Mr. Baryshnimoth smiled apologetically, saving me from what could have been a very sticky situation. "Don't worry about it," he said sweetly. "I couldn't shake your hand even in a pinch. You see, if I let go of this crutch I'll fall flat on my face."

At that moment I realized that the impostor had accidentally upstaged himself. It was curtains for him. "I'm afraid you've already fallen flat on your face." I smiled graciously. "And you don't even have a leg to stand on."

HOW DID INCOGNITO MOSQUITO
KNOW THAT THE SUPPOSED MIKHAIL
BARYSHNIMOTH WAS ACTUALLY AN
IMPOSTOR?

If he were the *real* Baryshnimoth with a *real* broken left leg, he would have carried a crutch under his left wing to support himself. So . . . he would have had no trouble extending his right wing for Incognito to shake.

The only way that the bug would have fallen over while shaking Incognito's hand is if he carried the crutch under his right wing—the wrong wing.

While the impostor had danced the performance of a lifetime—without ever lifting a toe—the time had come for him to bow out. Say for about twenty years.

I returned from lunch ahead of the rest of the class to brace myself for the afternoon session. I found Mosquito somersaulting across the classroom floor. "Just turning things over in my mind," he explained sheepishly. "In this business, everything has to be on the tip of your tongue. Of course, you have to be careful not to reveal top-secret info every time you lick an envelope. On the other hand, if you put your foot in your mouth, you can swallow your words in a hurry. See what I mean?

"Seriously though," the Mosquito continued as the rest of the class filed in. "You really do have to be on your toes. The Chief is always quizzing me, trying to trip me up. Of course, he'd deny it—says I trip up enough on my own. And he's always kidding. For example, he said to me just the other day, 'Mosquito, I don't know what makes you tick, but I wish it was a time bomb.'

"Without missing a beat, I shook my head and replied, 'Well, Chief, sorry to disappoint you. I guess you just can't teach an old bug new ticks!' Unfortunately the Inspector was not amused. He has a very short fuse, you know. It just goes to show you. You never know what to expect in this business. Take our next story, for example. Sometimes you just waltz in on a case and have a ball."

4
The Crushed Crashers Affair

It was one of the few nights that I wasn't out on the town. An old flame had recently flickered, leaving me to fend for myself. I'd planned a quiet evening at home. I relished the time to watch reruns of my favorite TV show, *S*Q*U*A*S*H*, broil a hamburger, and cat-sup on some reading.

I was just about to unlock my door with its thirteen ingenious security devices of my own invention, when my eye fell on an envelope lying on my doorstep. I bent down to pick it up—the envelope, not my eye. It was addressed to: I. Mosquito Esq. I was a little confused. I mean, I'm a bona fide mosquito, right? I'm not "mosquito-esque" in any way. Either you are a mosquito or you're not. You can't have it both ways!

Inside the envelope was a magnificently inscribed invitation that read:

Madame Emily Vanderbugs
kindly requests the presence
of
Mr. Incognito Mosquito, Private Insective
AT A GALA CHARITY BENEFIT
SPONSORED BY
Better Hives and Gardens
AT THE
Waldorf Wasporia Ballroom
IINS

I'll have to admit, I was puzzled. Although I'm missing a few pieces here and there, I'm not often puzzled. IINS? Was that French for RSVP? Just then a huge limo pulled up to my door. (Some trick considering I live on the thirty-third floor of an apartment building. I wonder how it got past the doorman.) Anyway, two economy-sized bodyguard types tried to stuff me into this car. Bodily! Then I understood. IINS— Immediately If Not Sooner!

"Just give me a minute, fellas!" I yelled over my shoulder as I threw on my tuxedo, cumberbug and all. I had some trouble buttoning up my ruffled shirt. You know how they have all those tiny buttons? Well, I kept having one left over at the end. Could I have lost a hole? Finally I decided to keep the leftover button for my lip in case of an emergency. Within minutes I was being whisked off to the Waldorf with all of the pieces in the proper places. Almost all of the pieces, anyway.

I found the Wasporia really decked out. I just couldn't take my eyes off the place. I was so busy observing that I neglected to observe the limo's window closing on my nose. Ooh! That's not smarts. However, now my nose matched my tux and my eyes— black and blue.

I was ushered into a parlor off the main ballroom and introduced to Madame Emily Vanderbug, Wasporia bigwig. My hostess hovered and fluttered around me. "Oh, Mr. Mosquito, I'm so terribly sorry about your

nose. It's not always like that, is it? Can I get you anything? A drink? Some Peasant Under Glass? A Flylenol perhaps?"

As long as she was offering, I asked for a wasperin and a glass of water. Out of courtesy to my hostess, I told her to hold the ice. I know from personal experience how long it takes to fit the cubes into those little holes in the tray. Then I settled down to listen to Mme. Vanderbug's story. Somehow notorious jewel bugglers had been slipping into a number of parties recently, disguised as guests. Mme. Vanderbug was afraid that the crashers might already have made an appearance at the Wasporia. My job was to find the culprits and remove them without attracting the attention of several *Flywitness News* cameras in attendance.

Right away the famous insective brain started running, clanking, whirring, as it were. I've been told that the noise comes

from the moving parts—mostly nuts. I guess it's a good thing that I don't have all my marbles, or the noise would be deafening.

I had only two questions for my hostess. First I needed a description of the bugglers. For instance, did she have any idea of how tall these thieves were. Second, could she introduce me to her guests as some long-lost uncle or something. Mme. Vanderbug answered both questions with a single lilting response—killing two bugs with one tone, so to speak. "Mr. Mosquito, everything is relative, and frankly I'd just as soon you weren't mine."

I nodded, still convinced that appearing as myself would be a mistake. A lot of people have told me that. I knew that at parties like this, the gossip was so thick you could spread it with a wife. Or a husband for that matter. So I decided to be introduced as the ruler of a tiny European country, the Prince of Monocle, and wore one just to prove my point. Though I've never understood why rich people wear monocles in the

first place. I mean, they can certainly afford
a whole pair of glasses. But, when in Italy,
do as the Italians do. So I did. I told the
other guests to just call me Squinty.

On entering the ballroom I could see that this affair was serious posh-city. We're talking monogrammed sugar cubes here. The guest list looked like a page out of *Who's What*. Clearly the bugs in this crowd all had a place on the social register—the social cash register, that is.

Apparently Mme. Vanderbug had her own suspicions as to the general locale of the dashing crashers. She steered me through the crowd toward a group of bugs engaged in lively conversation. First she introduced me to the evening's entertainment, famed hornet player Gnat King Cole. Having been a jitterbug from way back, I was awed. "Hey, man!" I crooned. "It don't mean a thing if it ain't got that sting. Doo-op, Doo-op. Slap me hive!"

Needless to say, Gnat was floored. After picking him up, I met the stately but ex-

tremely short Lord and Lady Wasply,
and Sir Cyril, Knight of the Garter Snake.
I made small talk to put them at knees—I
mean, at ease. "I hear the pound is shrink-
ing again. Good thing, too. It's very difficult
to be rich and British, you know. Carrying
around all those pounds can really weigh
you down. The richer you are, the shorter
you get. Nothing personal, you understand. Why, just last week I cashed a check
and went out of the bank looking like
the Hunchbug of Notre Dame."

71

"Oh, Pooh," responded the bug on my right, who turned out to be none other than A.A. Phid, author of that children's classic, *Now We Are Tix.*

But before I had a chance to respond, the Baron Von Roachschild shook my hand, introducing himself, his wife the Baroness, and his son, the Baronet Von Roachschild. Frankly, the boy seemed a bit uncooperative to me. He kept fiddling with his tie, which I guess would have been okay except the darn thing was out of tune. His mother apologized, explaining that her son was quite spoiled. "He was born with a silver spoon in his mouth, you see," she said.

Graciously I nodded. "Yes, it must be tough. All of the other children being born with tongues, I mean."

The last bug in our group turned out to be the Right Reverend P. Mantis. Would that have made him a Left Reverend if he

72

was standing on my other side? Naturally I didn't hesitate to ask him. You see, I believe religiously in treating bugs of the cloth just like everyone else. I'd just finished my question when all of a sudden the Right Reverend looked faint. I seem to have that effect on people for some reason. I helped him to a chair. "Can I get you a cassock for your feet? Help you loosen your collar? Would you like a piece of apple pious?" I vespered in his ear. However, the Honorable P.

Mantis insisted that he was fine, and that I return to the party. So I did.

Well, the introductions were over, and so was the party for the jewel thieves! I raised my hand to summons the local authorities but all I got were three local waiters. I realized that I would have to take matters into my own hands and personally deliver the bugglers to the police stationed at the Wasporia's entrance.

Smiling disarmingly, I whispered news of an exciting but highly confidential, not to mention illegal, business proposition into Baron Von Roachschild's ear. Motioning to his wife and son, the Baron maneuvered us toward the door, supposedly to discuss this deal in more detail.

"Swine before pearls," I said, smilingly holding the door open for my overconfident confidants.

"Age before beauty," Von Roachschild

beamed back, pushing me ahead.

"Thugs before bugs," I grinned evilly, pushing the entire family into the arms of the waiting police.

WHAT MADE INCOGNITO MOSQUITO SUSPECT THE VON ROACHSCHILDS?

Incognito Mosquito was not unfamiliar with nobility. He came from a long line of . . . long lines. So he knew that while the wife of a baron is indeed a baroness, a baron's son has no official title. The term *baronet* refers to the lowest inherited rank of nobility, but has no blood relation to either a baron or a baroness.

Blood may be thicker than water, but Incognito Mosquito could still see right through the Von Roachschilds. So much for nobility. Naturally the family was crest-fallen. Out of courtesy to their fallen crest, the family was assigned to the Residential Suite at Robber Baron's, the prison catering to in-mates of the in-crowd.

I think the sudden rush of applause from his starstruck students really stunned the Mosquito. "Thank you, thank you, thank me," he said blushingly. Incognito Mosquito clearly did not believe that modesty is the best policy. Apparently the students thought that this last case marked the end of the course. However, the Insective mistook the applause as a demand for an encore. He still had some words of wisdom to share with those more fortunate than himself. But first he decided to take questions from the audience.

One really preppy type, with more

alligators on his clothes than Tarzan wrestled in his entire lifetime, crocked his head and asked, "Professor Mosquito, you say that your time is never your own—that you're on call twenty-four hours a day."

"Sometimes twenty-five hours, like on leap year," the Mosquito added.

"So, sir, what I want to know is how can you ever relax? For example, do you close your eyes when you sleep?"

"Hmmm," commented the Insective, deep in thought. "That's a good question. Frankly, I've never stayed up long enough to find out!"

The next question came from a serious student in the back row. "Mr. Mosquito, I don't understand how you can live with the constant threat of death and destruction all the time. I mean, all that tension, all that violence, would drive me buggy— the knives, the guns, the threats on your life. How do you stand it? Can you answer that for me?"

"Well, I'll take a stab at it. Of course, my guessing what other private insectives feel is a shot in the dark, but as for me it's pretty cut and dried. Old Blood and Guts Mosquito, they call me. I've made out my last will and pestiment, leaving everything to posterity. I don't believe in looking behind me, as you can see. So that's basically it. I've prepared for my future; now all I have to worry about is my past. That about sums up my life. Next question please."

A young womanbug stood up. It was about time that somebody stood up to the Mosquito. "Can you tell us how you feel about women in the private insective game?"

"Frankly, my feeling used to be that women belong in the home—washing clothes, vacuuming, ironing, and attending to other pressing matters. However, even I, Incognito Mosquito, must change with the times. And I must admit, there have been times in my career when women have made very challenging opponents. Which coincidentally brings us to our last case . . ."

5
The Flying Jacket Racket

It was a glorious Sunday morning. You don't often get six in one month, you know. I'd decided to take the day off from painting my apartment to spend some time sunning at the beach. My mother always told me that a bug in the sand is worth two on the brush. If so, I figured I could open up a second office, do twice the business, and claim myself as a deduction on my own tax return. Deductive reasoning has always been one of my strong points.

Anyway, I'd just opened my beach reading, *The Catcher in the Pumpernickel,* when my beeper buzzed (buzzer beeped?). Calling into the office, I discovered that yet another case was waiting for me. It's tough to be a hot property. But duty called, so I grabbed a cab and headed for Beverly Anthills, a ritzy suburb on the outskirts

of town. Once again, it was back to the saltine mines.

Strange thing—the cab driver left the VACANT sign on the whole way there. Did he know something I didn't know? When he asked for a tip at the end of the ride, I told him Asparagus in the fourth. He pulled away so quickly that I left my hat in his cab and he left his door in my hands.

Without wasting a second I immediately looked around at my surroundings. I let out a sharp whistle. What a setup! Or should I say stickup? You see, this was the summer mansion of Maflia boss Sy the Fly, a legend in his own slime. Talk about security! This place had electrified fences, alarms, and vicious attack dogs. And that was just to protect the bodyguards. Before I knew it, I was being photographed, fingerprinted, checked, and searched. I asked if they'd throw in a haircut as long as they were at it. They said no, but they'd be glad to take a little off the top—say to the nose or so.

At last I was brought before my hosts, Sy the Fly and his wife, Lady Di. "Nice little mansion you've got here, Mr. and Mrs. Fly," I said admiringly.

"We like it. Be it ever so hovel, there's no place like home. Besides, it has eighty-three rooms and cost fifty-seven million

bucks," replied my hostess with the boastest.
"We even have a golf course."

"That's nice," I replied. "Although many
wealthy people have private golf courses."

"Inside?"

Ever the considerate one, Sy the Fly interrupted with, "Is der anyting I can do to make yous more comfortable?"

"Taking off these handcuffs with the built-in thumbscrews would be a good start," I answered with a smile.

"Okay. Now, let's get down to brass tacks here, Mosquito—" Sy the Fly began before I stopped him with, "Now that you mention it, I'd appreciate it if you'd remove those brass tacks from my chair. It would make sitting down much more pleasant."

Sy sneered. "Did anyone ever tell you that you're a pain in the ear, Mosquito?" (Interestingly enough, I think that's one of the few spots on the anatomy that I hadn't gotten to before.)

"Listen up, Mosquito," Sy the Fly said, "if yous know what's good for you. My adorable wife here and me, wees got a problem. It goes like dis."

"All right, Sy. I'll take over now," Lady Di interrupted. "Years ago I went to Camp Marvae Larvae with the soon-to-become-famous flier, Amelia Earwig. We were both just little buglettes, you see, but very good friends and bunkmates. As a token of her esteem for me, Ms. Earwig gave me one of her childhood flying jackets. So far, so good?"

I knodded knowingly.

"Well, a while later, say twenty years or so, Amelia Earwig asked to borrow back the jacket to take some photographs. And wouldn't you know it, she disappeared off the face of the earth before returning the jacket to me."

"What a shame. Such a waste. An incredible tragedy," I said sadly.

"Yeah," Sy added. "And da jacket was almost brand-new. But the story has a happy ending . . ."

"Wow! You mean, after fifty years they've found Amelia Earwig?" I yelled.

"No, no! Even better than that!" Mrs. Fly smiled. "They've found the jacket. Sy and I went and looked at it very carefully. We even brought one of our stooges—um, ah— I mean, scientific experts to check it out. We're sure it's the same jacket. Why, there's even a camp nametag in the collar that reads 'Diana Fly' as plain as the nose on your face.

Well, maybe not quite as plain."

"I'll overlook that remark," I said good-naturedly. "I only wish I could overlook this nose. But wait a minute, Di. I don't understand what the big deal is with this jacket racket."

"Oh, just a minor detail, Mosquito. It seems the jacket is worth a lot of money, since it originally belonged to dear Amelia and all," Lady Di explained. "The authorities are claiming that the jacket is a national treasure. A regular gold mine!"

"Ridiculous, ain't it?" Sy continued. "A gold mine. Now wees all know dat Lady Di wants de jacket back for purely senti*metal* reasons, don't we? But the authorities won't release the jacket until we can prove that it definitely belongs to Di. So dat's why you're here."

Just as Sy the Fly and Lady Di finished,

MONA FLEASA

the parlor door swung open. You could have dressed my toes in a pair of rubber hose. Standing before me was one of the greatest insectives ever hatched, Sam Spud, Potato Bug. What a cool character! I was honored to be in his presence. I would even have been honored to be in his absence. He spoke. "Hello, Mosquito."

"Oh, wow! You know my name."

"Naturally," Sam Spud replied. "It's my business to know, and I also know you're on the Ten Most Unwanted List. You come between measles and four broken legs. What I don't understand, Mosquito, is what the devil you're doing here. I mean, your being here is as ridiculous as trying to go up Fliagara Falls without a paddle. Not to mention a barrel. Listen, Sy, it was bad enough that you kidnapped me. All in all, I'd rather be in Casablanca, if you get my drift. But bringing in Incognito Mosquito to second-guess me!!!"

"Nnnoww, you listen here, Potato Bug," I spuddered. "It may be true that you're one of the greatest private insectives of all time, and that you were called in on this case first. But I'm no masher—I mean crasher. So don't you go off half baked."

"You know, I never thought I'd find myself apologizing to you," Sam Spud replied. "I'm just not myself. But I guess as long as I'm not yourself, I'm okay. What I'm trying to say is I'm sorry, Mosquito. I guess when they knocked me on the head to bring me here, it dazed me. I must feel about as confused as you are naturally," Sam Spud concluded accurately. "But I'll tell you this," the Potato Bug continued. "If you can solve this jacket caper, I'm all eyes."

"Yes, Mosquito," Di Fly chimed in impatiently. "I want everyone to know that jacket is mine—or my name isn't Diana Fly!"

I smiled self-confidently. Sam Spud may be the greatest insective ever hatched, I thought to myself, but when they made me, they broke the Jell-O mold. And would you believe it, even as I was thinking, the solution to this puzzling mystery was already beginning to gel in my mind. I saw how to get both myself and Sam Spud out of this jam.

Well, I figured this was my big moment. I decided to make the most of it. Turning to my waiting audience, I addressed the Potato Bug first. "Sham, shweetheart, this is going to knock your shocks off. Sit down."

Smiling, I turned to my two pigeons, who thought they were about to get a nest egg, but in a moment might try to fly the coop. "Sy the Fly and Lady Di, you've restored my faith in crooked racketeers, mobsters, and gangland gangsters everywhere. Tell me, are your screwples loose? I ask because we all know that there's no way that jacket belongs to you."

HOW DID INCOGNITO MOSQUITO KNOW
THAT SY THE FLY AND LADY DI HAD
NO CLAIM TO AMELIA EARWIG'S JACKET?

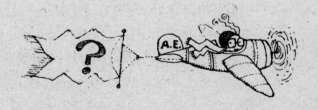

Lady Di Fly claimed that Amelia Earwig had given her the jacket when they were childhood bunkmates at Camp Marvae Larvae. She proved it by telling Incognito about the nametag in the collar.

But all the nametag did was to name Lady Di and husband Sy the Fly as frauds. The nametag had her married name on it! Incognito concluded that their stooge—alias scientific expert—must have quickly sewn the tag into the jacket when he was allowed to inspect it. In other words, Sy the Fly and Lady Di hanged themselves with their own thread.

Incidentally, the Flys did not go un-punished. Sam Spud, Potato Bug, had something to say to them about that, namely: "Just remember this. A hiss is but a hiss. A Sy is but a Fly. And if I ever catch you trying

something like this again, I'll pull your lower lip so far above your head you'll think you're wearing a beret. And that's the name of that tune."

And it was too.

Deafening applause signaled the lecture's end. As Incognito Mosquito, Private Insective, bid a fond farewell to the class, it looked like the close of another fascinating day in the life of this reporter. Actually, I guess I shouldn't complain. My last story on the famed Insective earned me a promotion. Now I'm not only a cub reporter for a great metropollen newspaper, I also bring in the coffee.

Even so, assigning me to another Incognito Mosquito story seemed to be adding insult to injury—slime to punishment, if you get my jest. See? I was already beginning to talk like him. Wait until I started to write like him! It would serve my editor right. I mean, just because she wanted our underground newspaper to do a groundbreaking story on educating crimefighters is no reason to stick me with the digging. Now here I was, up to my knees in Mosquito and sinking fast. Just because I'm low man on the totem pole everyone thinks they can sit on me.

I had a few last questions for the Insective before turning in my report. But by the time I'd collected my notes and my thoughts, he was gone. I found out that the Mosquito's next assignment was to demonstrate the fine art of undercover work* to a group of young FBI bedbugs. Arriving at the address I'd been given, a dingy alley, I discovered the bedbugs blanketed with garbage. It was quite a spread! Sleeze-city!

I couldn't see the Insective anywhere. He fit right in. Silently I prayed that the garbage bugade would pick up the whole lot, rescuing me from this crazy story I'd been sent on. Unfortunately the trashman didn't cometh.

I called out to the Mosquito but he didn't answer. What luck! I was about to give up when I heard a rustling in a garbage can behind me. It stirred up a huge cloud of dust. I'd just taken out my handkerchief to relieve my stuffed nose when the top of the can lifted slightly, revealing an all too familiar pair of antennae.

"Shhh!" the can's lone occupant hissed. "You want to blow my cover?"

I nearly flipped my lid. Naturally it was Incognito Mosquito, in the flesh—and under my skin. Talk about scraping the bottom of the barrel!

"You don't really want to write about me, do you?" the trashee said.

"I don't, but I will," I answered. I had no intention of surrendering my notes to the Insective for the sake of preserving his "incognitohood," as he'd convinced me to do the last time I'd attempted to write an article on him. And I told him so.

"Don't be ridiculous," the Mosquito replied generously while flicking an orange rind off his lapel. "Just because your article will expose me for what I really am? Why should that upset me? Of course you realize that you'll also expose dozens of criminals to serious humiliation in the process. Totally ruin their reputations. And you won't do much for the victims either.

Quelle fromage," Mosquito commented, pulling a piece of cheese off his sleeve. "Frankly, I think it's muensterous. But I guess if you gouda do it, you gouda do it. It's a feta accompli. So let's cut all this cheddar and get down to business."

It took only a few minutes to get the information I needed from the Insective. "Well, I'm glad to see you're taking this like a bug, Mosquito," I said.

"Do I have a choice? Incidentally, if I were you, I'd make a copy of those notes as soon as I could. You never know what can happen. Better to be safe than sorry."

"Thank you, Mosquito. I think that's a very good idea. Any idea where I might—"

"FBI headquarters lobby. First door on your left. I've got to get going now. Looking forward to reading your article." As suddenly as he'd appeared, Incognito

Mosquito vanished back inside his trash can. Ashes to ashes, trash to . . . etc. and so forth, as they say.

I followed his directions to the copying machine. After depositing my change, laying out my notes, and pushing all the proper buttons, I sat down to wait. By the time I realized what was happening, it was too late. The machine had already swallowed up my entire stack of notes as it began to spit out the first sheet—shredded into dozens of strips! I realized that Incognito Mosquito had directed me not to the nearest copying machine, but to the nearest paper shredder.

But there was nothing I could do. I had been stung again. All I was left with was a pile of spaghetti confetti. And the knowledge that somewhere, somehow, sometime, when he least expected it, Incognito Mosquito, Private Insective, would have a taste of his own medicine—where it hurt.

In the meantime, I managed to reconstruct these stories so that you can remember them. After all, why should I be the only one walking around with this annoying buzz in my ear all the time?

About the Author

E. A. Hass shares a New York City apartment with two lazy, literate cats. In the summer there are usually several dozen mosquitoes around as well, any one of which could be *the* mosquito.

E. A. wears as many hats as Incognito Mosquito wears disguises. Book author, magazine writer, bookstore manager, sometime illustrator, publicist—Hass has done it all. And more: E. A. also appears as Dr. Book on American Public Radio's *Paging Dr. Book* show, giving kids advice on reading and prescriptions for good books. Readers of Incognito Mosquito always feel better.

About the Artist

Don Madden lives with his wife, son, and daughter in an old farmhouse in upstate New York. They share the place with a large scraggly dog and a small flabby cat, who spend their time trading fleas. Before moving to the country Mr. Madden studied and taught at the Philadelphia Museum College of Art. Now he illustrates children's books and fights off hordes of six-legged visitors.